Paradise and Murders and Such
The Final Case

Three detectives retire to a paradise place (Well, one was already there) and unite to try to solve a difficult case.

Contents

About the author

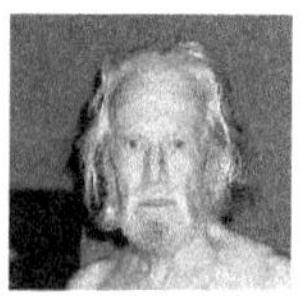

CD began writing fiction in 1984 and has more than 300 books published as of 3/15/16 in SciFi, murder, orchid culture and various other fields.

He now resides Gualaca, Chiriqui, Panamá, where he continues research into epiphytic plants and plays music with friends. He loves the culture of the indigenous people and counts a majority of his closer friends among that group. He funds those he can afford through the universities where they have all excelled. "The Indios are very intelligent people, they are simply too poor (in material things and money.) to pursue higher education."

CD loves Panamá and the people, despite horrendous experiences (Free e-book; *Fading Paradise*). He plans to spend the rest of his life in the paradise that is Panamá

CD is involved in research of natural cancer cure at this time. It has proven effective in all cases, so far. It is based on a plant that has been in use for thousands of years, is safe, available, and cheap. He was cured of a serious lymphoma with use of the plant, *Ambrosia peruviana.*

Information about this cure is free on the FaceBook page Ambrosia peruviana for cancer. CD asks only that all who try it please report on its effectiveness on that group.

Paradise and Murder and Such

The Deal

CD Grimes, PI, billionaire, signed the titulo. Alma, his wife, signed. CD gave Emilio Fuentes the check for one point five million dollars. They went to the caja to pay the notary fee, shook hands, and Fuentes got in his car and left.

"Done deal!" CD declared to Alma. "We now own that chunk of paradise!"

"CD, I never really believed there was a perfect place for us. This is it!

"I'm so glad we met Clint and learned about it. I'll miss Dave here, is all. He was half-crazy and weird, but we went all over this place for orchids. I think I'll have the most complete collection of native orchids of Panamá in the world. He left me the three places he made gardens. I have that place in Calderas for the really high altitude types. The island has a peak at six hundred meters, so the warm and intermediate ones will do well there. The comarca's two hundred sixty meters away. They'll inherit the place. He has more than eight hundred species there.

"We can live in that house there until we have a place built. I guess you'll want an underground cold house."

"No. We have the place in Calderas. I doubt I'll do a lot more with hybrids of those types. Maybe it would be better to leave those things in the states. We can spend ten lifetimes doing the kinds of things Dave and you were working on. I'm more and more into that."

"Okay. We also have a deal on other things. The business is now in the hands of the kids. They run things without your interference. They learned how to keep on top of the government and all that from you. They aren't interested in the detective bit, so I guess the CD Grimes Detective Agency is another thing of the past.

"CD, I think we've both been able to make a mark on the world. Dave and Clint and the Stories think exactly like we do. We fit together, and we fit this place. We've always had a philosophy more like the Indios than what passes for 'normal' in the society we're finally able to escape completely.

"We have to work out some way for Nick and Janet to come here. Clint isn't far a good part of the time. Cusapín is only thirty kilometers away. They both love the country and the lifestyle. Nick has had his fill of the kinds of greedy crime he's worked with. It's too true in the states that it's a ratrace where the rats are winning."

"I've talked with Nick. He's already agreed that he would like nothing better, but he has some kind of hang-up because we can afford this kind of thing, while he's a cop with a cop's salary. He'll get the pension and his Social Security and has a few dollars in the bank. I've got Pancho DeGulio and JK convincing him to come.

"I want Pancho to come. He says he'll spend part of his time here, but he can't stay for long. If he's here those gangsters he's reformed would start wondering if they could take over from ... that's not true. Others would move in.

"All our friends will be welcomed. I doubt their psychologies would let them be content with this kind of life.

"Well, I want to talk with Clint while I'm here. This is close. I think he and Tyna would like to live out here. He's worried about becoming useless on the comarca, though that won't ever happen. He's almost eighty and in better health and condition than most people in their thirties. His kids have made names for themselves, same as ours and Nick's.

"Cole, Nick's son, is making a big splash with his forensics research."

"Clint's, Nito, is making a great name in police procedures. He's modernized the Policia Nacionál to where most in the states are using his techniques. If it wasn't for the corruption in the courts, this country would be the envy of the Americas! Nicole married an Indio and is making a name in medicine. She's running all those hospitals and clinics Clint and Manny built."

"I'll let you stay here with Tyna and Clint. I'll talk with Clint, then go back to Florida to get things settled and have what you want sent. I won't bring much, myself."

"I made a list and gave it to the kids. It's not a whole lot. The paperwork and all that sort of thing is all on flash drives. There's some equipment and a few personal items. It'll be the first time in my life I've moved where I didn't need a convoy to carry the crap! Everything will fit on the plane, and you'll have room for four passengers to top it.

"CD, try to make Nick and Janet two passengers, okay? Janet and I click, and you and Nick click. All of us click with Clint and Tyna."

"I'll give it a go!"

"Clint, we really would like for you and Tyna to live there at least part of the time. Alma and Tyna get along as well as we do. I'm going to try to get Nick and Janet to come here. Nick's ready to retire. We all think alike on major issues. We've all spent most of our lives setting up others to have something. It's time we had a little bit for ourselves. We've got money up the ass, but not much that really matters.

"I'm speaking mostly for me. You have a life I envy the hell out of. What you always warn about has happened to me. I don't have the money, it has me.

"More than that, I'm talking about Tyna and Janet and Alma. You know they've gone through a lot for us. It's time to give them something back. Money ain't it. They've got more than they know what to do with. Tyna loves this kind of place. It's a lot like the comarca, but without the pressures of the comarca. Alma loves it. It's where she can do the things that she really wants to do. She won't have to run away from anything to do that here. Janet can be in a place where she doesn't have to agonize over her husband being a cop on violence detail. She won't spend her life with the dread of opening the door to find two cops with black armbands who come to break the news to her.

"Okay. Tyna will have fifty Indios living on the island. It's big enough. There are four families living there now. I told them they could stay as long as they like. You know what I mean. We get along very well. Alton has that place and fishes. He can supply us with seafoods and we'll supply him and family with whatever they need. Berto is already growing cacao and coffee here. And a lot of other things. We'll be totally self-sufficient here."

Clint thought about it. He was seventy nine and in very good health and condition. Tyna was as healthy, but they could both use less pressure. They had made that pressure a part of their lives deliberately, but that was when they were thirty years younger.

"I think I could go for that, but Tyna won't want a fancy house or those kinds of trappings."

"Alma and I are sick to death of that shit, ourselves. Basic, but comfortable. One room I don't ever have to go into with the things that are likely to come up because of the business and so forth. Alma's happy in a tent in the jungle. I only want a clean comfortable place. I like to sit on the porch and watch the sunrises and sunsets."

"Deal!"

CD's phone rang. He was expecting two calls. This one was from Pancho DeGulio, one of the most powerful people in the world, when it came to the mobs – not because of anything he did, but because of what he knew.

"CD here. It's your dime."

"A call costs a quarter, locally. This isn't locally," Pancho replied. "How are things in Panamá?"

"Better than I deserve. I want to ask you for a couple of favors having to do with this place."

"So? Ask!"

"I bought an island on the border of the comarca. I'm moving here with Alma. Clint and Tyna are going to live there. I want you and Nick and your families to move here.

"I know your situation. I know you can't stay long at a time, but I want you to have a place here. Your wife and family can stay, too.

"I want you to convince Nick and Janet. They want to come, but feel they would be out of place. We're all millionaires. We really do want them here. It will be strictly basic. We'll live more like the comarca lifestyle. No greed or materialism, and no laying around being a bum."

"I will see. I think Nick knows he's really the same as you. I'll speak with him."

"I'm coming back to Florida tomorrow. I'd like for you and your family and Nick and Janet to come back here with me."

"I will be unable to come for about two months. Perhaps I can convince Nick to retire and go back with you. The only reason he hasn't retired already is because he would have nothing to do. That isn't a position any of our little group could tolerate for more than a week."

"We have a deal! Paradise, and we don't even have to die to get here!"

*

Det. Lt. Nick Storie (*) had a method that had worked well for much of his career. He was a problem solver. He would locate the point where what he needed to know was, then go directly there. He wondered how that would affect his new life. He would simply have to find new kinds of problems to solve. He ended up friends with most of the top gangsters in the states. They respected him as a man whose honor was unquestionable. He even ended up friends with many he caught. He might even agree with parts of it, but his sworn job was to catch them. What the courts and lawyers did past that point wasn't his decision to make.

"Nick, I didn't say anything. I know it's your decision, but I'm so thrilled we're going to be able to live down there I can't hope to describe it! Alma and Tyna are the very two people in this world I can relate to completely. We think very much alike. We like to do things, even though they're different kinds of things for each of us. Alma wants to tramp all over the jungle, Tyna wants to be with the people on the comarca, I want to write a book! I've wanted to write a book for years and never could get started. Whenever I think of a way, something happens to make me wait another day, then I don't.

"I believe the book won't be so dark, there. Here, it would be about fighting and arguing and doing whatever else it takes to accomplish something that would be just plain silly down there. Maybe I can write something worth reading."

"You want to write a book? Too bad Dave's not around anymore. He wrote two or three hundred books!"

"I know. He's where I got the idea."

The caller vibrated. He looked at it.

"Well, I turned in my resignation/retirement today. I get home and get a call.

"My last case assignmnet for South Station, Naples, Florida! I hope I can solve it tonight so we can start packing in the morning! Enough is too much!"

"Yeah, right, and uh-huh!"

He kissed her soundly and headed for his car.

**

Clint Faraday, PI, Retired, (**) was a legwork type with a mind that sought the surest way through a situation. He had also learned to be pragmatic about a lot of things. Things that served well in the USA were just plain silly and extreme here. The older he got, the more he fell into the Indigeno thought pattrerns about many things.

"Clint! It's Rojelio, at Chiriqui Grande!" Tyna called. Clint answered the phone.

"Clint? Que tal? Got a bit of a problem here. I would appreciate your help. It's the kind of thing you're so good at. Two people killed in a traffic accident that wasn't."

"How was it done? Who?"

"Car went over the side just above Cañastas. No skid marks. In neutral. Brakes working. Head wounds not consistent with any surface they might have met. Man and wife. Campbells. Mid-fifties. From Nevada. Tourists. Didn't have much money. No alcohol or drug use. Staying in Bocas, on the island. Seemed suspicious and were hiding something or from something.

"I studied police procedures under Nito. That's basically what you need? I haven't spent much time on it. It happened last night, about seven thirty."

"I'll go to Isla Colón. I'll see what I can see."

Page 6

***

CD Grimes, PI, (***) was a billionaire who had rejected a lot of the lifestyle of those people in the USA. Most money people were, to him, greedy, empty, boring things. He couldn't divest himself of Crane because of contracts with the military and government agencies. To simply close down Crane would put three thousand people out of work overnight. He had managed to put most of that on Tony Jacobi, who had, for years, been the real head of Crane.

CD had become famous, in a way, in Florida. He went through the courses about police work and law, was for many years a semi-official deputy sheriff and a state marshal for the grand jury (which he didn't believe had a legitimate place in law, in his earlier years). He used his position to have a lot of things done for him. His security clearances and certifications were honestly earned. He believed in what he was doing until it got so out of hand.

He was considered pompous and arrogant until you got to know him. It was his method. He convinced himself that, without any doubt whatever, he would solve any case he took. So far, most of that was successful.

The world had changed radically in the past fifty years. CD had changed a little bit. His ideas clashed with what was considered as acceptable now. Money had bought out honor in too much of the world. He was an honorable man, as were Nick and Clint. That was their real connection.

CD got out of the Jeep at the Crane plant to go to his son's office. A woman was just leaving, so he went in.

"Hi, Dad! So you're really going to abandon us with this mess?"

"Yeah, CD. I had Tony to run things until you were ready. I've said before that you would be smart to find someone like him to screw things up!"

"Tony Jacobi screw things up? You're joking, of course! He

spent half his time unscrewing things you'd made a mess of!"

Well, you can work out a system to screw things up. JK can undo it. He's the one who runs things, anyhow."

"He had two senators and two reps here to whine and beg. I don't know what it was about, but they made some kind of deal where that bunch retired for personal and health reasons. I guess their replacements will be as bad or worse.

"Oh! Fred Hampton called. He wants you to call him as soon as you have a spare moment."

"Fred Hampton?"

"He said he knew you from the orchid society. I suppose it will be about that."

"You have to see to all those things now, you know. I'm not about to take three acres of orchids to a place where you see them naturally, no matter where you look!"

"Sis will handle that. She's into them. I'm not. My brother is, more than me."

CD nodded and took the phone to call the number CD (His son) gave him. Hampton answered. He said CD was known as a detective in murder cases. There was a murder in his family. The police wouldn't even investigate it!

"Okay. I only have a day or two, but I'll look into it. Meet me at Sancho's Mexican in thirty minutes? It's lunch time. I want to tell all of them there goodbye. I'm moving out of the states."

*

"Hi, Larry. What's up? You called for me to assist?" Larry Feng was a good cop. Nick had arranged for him to go into police work twenty years ago. He worked several stations and was now head of violent crimes, South Station. Nick had turned down the position four times. He wasn't the administrator type. That's what the position required.

"It might not be much, but you can usually spot things that

everyone else will miss.

"Remember, back in about ninety four, when you introduced me to Greco? That crazy Mexican woman who wanted to establish a chain of whorehouses here?" (Nick Storie book13: *Trigger Happy/Strange Fish*)

"Lord, yes! That was something. It could have ruined the Olympic Games in Atlanta!"

"Greco called me. He asked if you could check into something for him here. It has to do with that. Candida got out of the pen, after serving the twenty years. The one you called Jojo didn't get any reduction. Not a good prisoner.

"She got out three days ago. She was sent directly to Mexico. Mexico wanted Jojo extradited there. He was supposed to be a witness ... well, who cares. He was to testify against her. He was being transferred to Miami. He had to come here to get an extradition order in the place where he was convicted."

"And he was hit," Nick finished.

"Pancho will know all about it. You can talk to him, nobody else can. Greco may be able to tell you something."

Nick sighed deeply and picked up the phone to call Greco, in Detroit, who conferenced with Artie Doniletti in New York. Mo Jefferson, the other major crime lord (now gone legitimate) Nick knew, had died of cancer two years ago. Julia Bocci, now Julia Doniletti, was in the hotel business, and had been involved in that case.

"What's the skinny, Greco?" Nick asked, when all were on the line.

"Short and sweet. Candida's out. Jojo was hit. He would tie her ass in a knot in Mexico. Who and how arranged? We do not want that one around, even as close as Mexico. None of us want to go back to the old days. We don't arrange hits anymore, or it would be a non-issue already."

"It will be someone she met while in the pen. It was

arranged there, probably. Where was she held?"

"Raiford. Artie checked that out."

"She had three people she was palsy with in the can," Artie said. "One is still there. She couldn't arrange anything. One is in Texas, and one is in Mexico as her guest. She's there."

"She could arrange it like we're doing. Talking on the phone. Whoever did it was damned professional, I'm guessing, if they hit him while in custody," Nick replied. "There's one person who might have a direction. I'll call Pancho.

"Guys, I'm retired from the police thing here. I'm moving to Panamá. CD is going, too. There's a retired detective from Florida, the Tampa area, who's got a place where we'll all live. On a paradise island in the Caribbean. It's pure heaven!"

They all wished him well. They would stay in touch. If they could arrange a vacation, they'd visit.

Nick called Pancho. They discussed the case. Pancho would get a request for information out. They then talked about the Panamá place.

Nick thought about this case, sighed again, and sent a request for information to the holding facility. He got a quick response. Jojo was hit from a distance with a high-powered rifle shot. One inch above the right ear. Definitely a professional job.

He then used the computer to get all information he could about Candida's stay in Raiford. They had it ready because of the hit, so it came in fast. He saw the three closest friends and that they were immediately checked. None could have done it, not to mention they weren't the type who would.

Visitors. One name seemed familiar. Sam Levin. Two visits, both in the last month.

Sam Levin and hits. What about that old case where the Cuban woman was hit just that way? Wasn't he suspected? Didn't he get a conviction ... it was his girlfriend. Her name was Gina Samosini. She was doing twenty to life.

But he was a suspected hit man.

Nick called Raiford to ask about Gina Samosini. She was there. She had some contact with Candida. Not much.

One short conversation would be enough.

Nick called Pancho and asked about Levin and Samosini. There was a silence, then, "Nick, you never fail to amaze me! I would never connect Levin with Candida, but his girlfriend ... and he visited her at Raiford. When?"

"Twice. Last month on the twenty second and on the twenty eighth. Candida already knew she was going to get out and be sent to Mexico. She could have fifty ways to learn Jojo was going to squeal."

"His address is listed on the visitor's list. See if he was anywhere he could have done it. If he was, case solved!"

Nick soon hung up and called Raiford one last time. Levin was in Sarasota. An hour away by car or bus on I-4.

Nick called in to Larry to say to check on where Sam Levin was at the time of the hit, find anyone who can say he was in that area, arrest him, and contact Mexico. Levin could make a deal to testify in Mexico that Candida paid him to eliminate the person who would make her conviction there a definite thing or he could face M-1 charges here. His choice.

"We're going to miss you and your connections here!" Larry said. "One of them will always know about anything vaguely related to their business."

"Not in this case, Lare. They didn't know where to look. If I hadn't had those two unrelated cases where certain people were involved I wouldn't have seen the connection. It would have to go to the unsolvable file: Mobs."

"Nobody else would have seen the connection, even if they were involved in those two cases. You would. That's why you were so good."

"I still am. I just don't want to spend the rest of my life

doing this. I'm going to Panamá."

Larry grinned and gave him the old one finger salute.

**

"Jelio, I have to know a lot more about the Campbells. I've checked them out, here in Bocas. There are some huge gaps in what I've learned, so far. It smells like a WP deal or something. The Campbells, these, didn't exist six years ago. I can't find much with the system that's worked so well for the past fifteen years. That means someone has gone to one hell of a lot of trouble to erase information from the web.

"It's not possible to erase it all. I have to check a few things. One thing will be certain, if it's WP or not. They weren't from Nevada. They'd probably never been near there. My connections to the old mobs don't have a clue.

"I'd say to forget it if some odd things hadn't been mentioned. Things that involve Panamá. Things that could even involve the comarcas. Things that could involve ... a lot of things.

"Jelio, they were very damned important to something. It could be something very nasty.

"I'll try to find the one who offed them, just to be able to find who hired him. I have a very good idea who that might have been, among three.

"You said the transmission was in neutral? Prints on the shift knob?"

"Wiped clean. Another reason we know it was no accident."

"Then I'm ninety percent certain I can find the one who did it. I think I can get information from him. I have a lever."

They talked a few minutes, then Clint took his boat to Almirante, where he asked if Tigre was back there.

No. He didn't think he would be. He asked that so he could throw some other names around that would make others think he didn't know who he was after.

"Evan Roberts? He went back to Costa Rica."

"Martín? Last I heard he was in Las Tablas – which thrills the shit out of people there, I suppose."

"Anderson? He's around somewhere. Chiriqui Grande last week."

"Arauz? Benito? Darien."

So. It was who he thought. Anderson. He had money now, so would be in David, at the casinos.

Clint took his boat to Chiriqui Grande, got his car, and headed for David. Anderson had been there a couple of nights ago, then had left. Probably to Panamá City.

Clint got a flight. Anderson had stayed in David, done the job, and took the money to head for the city and the big casinos – where he'd lose it all.

Clint checked into the Hotel California. Anderson would hit the casinos at about ten if he held to his pattern.

Eleven fifteen. The Grande Game. He was at the bar with his hooker for the night. Clint went to say he needed a quick word, then he could get back to his girlfriend.

Anderson knew him from a case before. A case where he had sent two people over the side of a mountain in a car with the transmission in neutral. Due to who they were, he let it slide, but had warned Anderson that he left prints on the gearshift knob. As soon as he heard the knob was wiped clean, he was sure it would be Anderson.

"Who paid? That's all I have to know."

"I don't know. Two grand up front, then two more when it was done. Voice on the phone. Money appeared by my door in a dirty paper bag when I got home, then inside an open window on the floor when I did the job. All I got was a note that they would look me up if they needed more contract work."

"Got the note?"

He reached in his pocket and handed Clint a typed note:

Aces, Pedro. I will look you up if and when more contract work is needed.

"Thanks. Get back to your whore before some other mark gets her eye."

"Thirty others here. Like I give a shit?"

"They call you Pedro?"

"No."

Clint grinned and went out. He went back to Chiriqui Grande in the morning. He told Rojelio it was a professional job and there wouldn't ever be enough evidence to convict anybody.

He was a bit curious. He would check into it some more. Later. He went back to Cusapín.

***

CD looked over the bunch at the restaurant. That was Hampton, to the side. He went over. Hampton waved to the other seat. He ordered tamales and tacos.

"What's it about?"

Fred shrugged. "My cousin was shot in the back of the head. George Bender. He wasn't using drugs, but it was execution style. He didn't even know any of those kinds. He was into religion, much more than I ever was. The police say it was obviously a drug-related execution, proven by the way it was done. They say all they can do is hope somebody says something, then they don't have much chance of getting a conviction.

"We all tried to tell them he was the last person on Earth who would ever have anything whatever to do with drugs. They said a lot of people have that reputation. If it had been true, he wouldn't be executed that way.

"Don't you wish cops were actually like those on CSI and New York Law or whatever?"

CD shook his head. He agreed that law was becoming more

and more a joke. Drugs were blamed for everything.

"Tell me as much as you know about what he was doing and where and with whom."

"He was into evangelical work, which means he would knock on your door and ask if you knew Jesus was your lord and savior and that kind of thing. He would try to convert you to the Church of Absolute Truth So There! or whatever.

"He really was honest with it. It was what he truly believed. I shouldn't put him down for it. He was the type you wanted to toss off the property, but no one would want to hurt him. I just don't get it!"

"He would go into neighborhoods and knock on doors. That kind. He was devout in his beliefs.

"Do you know which neighborhoods he was working?"

"Those closest to where his church was, I would imagine. He would sometimes go out to the island. He said there were more people there who were lost than in most areas. Most of those had a maid to answer the door and tell him to take a hike, so he didn't try ... he did say he saw something on Ana Mariah that troubled him deeply. Something about corrupting the youth, leading them astray. He saw something. A lot of lost souls who needed direction. He was going to speak with them about it or report it to someone or something."

"When?"

"About ten days ago. It was toward the causeway, I know. He said it was an ostentatious shrine to Satan.

"Yes! He said there was a yacht at the dock that shouldn't be there and that a lot of teenagers were partying on it! There was some fancy Italian car in the drive and a lot of BMW's and Lexuses and those kind of things."

"A yacht that shouldn't have been there? That could mean something. Did he say why it shouldn't have been there?"

There was a pause. "I'm trying to remember. We all sort of tune him out when ... a leader ... no, a ... politician of some sort, I think. I may be pissing up a rope, but I think it was something like that."

"I'll look into it, but won't have much time. I'm moving out of the states. If I can find anything, I know which cop to have go after it. I can't promise anything except that I *will* look into it."

They talked for a bit more. CD said his cousin had probably confronted the wrong kind of people. If they thought he was threatening them, exactly what had happened would happen.

They had the meal, CD told his friends there he was leaving, then went to the old Jeep he liked to drive. He was a billionaire who rode around in a restored WWII Jeep! And piloted his own six seater jet.

He drove out to the causeway and found what had to be the house. After talking to several near neighbors' housekeepers and yardmen, he knew which house. Two had seen a yacht at the dock more than once. Yes, there were a lot of young teenagers hanging around. The people in the house didn't have any children. There was booze, if not worse. Draw your own conclusions.

One said the name on the yacht was Dare2Bea.

A check of the records said the Dare2Bea was leased to a state attorney's aide.

CD asked, "A state attorney's aide makes enough to lease a yacht'?"

"Not as a state attorney's aide. Maybe he moonlights."

"She. Adelaide Farndon."

"Makes it on the fringe benefits. Sells a little ass. Frugal with the housekeeping money."

CD laughed, said the whole world had gone to hell, and went to his laptop to find out what he could about Adelaide Farndon. It seems she was from an independantly wealthy family, living part time in Miami and part time in Mexico City and part time in Cali, Colombia. She handled all appointments and assignments and court dates. She selected which judge would handle which case. Things like that.

Well, DUH! I can't see anything wrong there!

CD Grimes was a state marshal for many years. He still held the papers. He would arrange something. It would not be handled by locals. It was Saturday night. A very likely time for something to be going down.

CD's boat, the Nicely Done Too, came up the channel and stayed just outside the fancy yacht at the dock. There were a dozen or so teenage boys and girls on the deck of the Dare2Bea, dancing to a small live band and drinking beer and booze supplied on a decktop bar.

Two carloads of special police stopped in front and went to the front door, where they were denied entrance by a couple of overmuscled hoods. They shoved the hoods aside, two cops patted them down and put them in handcuffs. They went in.

Four of the police went onto the deck and waved to CD, who came alongside and boarded.

A rather fiery attractive woman came rushing from the master cabin to demand what was going on.

"It's called a raid," CD answered. "It seems there are a few underage citizens imbibing in strong alcoholic beverages supplied by a bar on the deck."

A cop came to whisper to him. He said to arrest everyone on the boat and in the house. He turned toward the woman to say, "And marijuana and cocaine are being used by those same minors, which means I sieze all properties associated with the illegalities as state marshal. I advise that you say nothing without benefit of counsel. Anything you say will be held against you in a court of law.

"Sgt. Adams, I think you will have to call for two or three more paddy wagons, huh?"

"At least!"

"Look! We can explain this! I want to talk to you in private!" the woman cried. "I have to make a couple of calls. This will all blow over in ten minutes, I promise!"

"You can make one call, after processing," Adams said. "Let's go!"

"You could end up cut crab bait, shithead!" she snarled. "You wouldn't be the first!"

"She just admitted to murder!" CD cried, aping shock.

"Fuck you! You don't know who you're going up against!"

"He's CD Grimes. You're A. Farndon. No lawyer in this state and forty nine others doesn't know who CD Grimes is! You think you're going to scare him, think again! He can buy and sell your whole cartell ten times over, and he's squeaky clean," Adams said, conversationally.

"ER! CD, er, what ... oh, shit!"

"That about covers it. Let's go."

Adams slapped the cuffs on her and started toward the dock, almost dragging her. She was very colorful in her choice of obscenities. CD said he'd go to the station to make out the afidavit he would see was followed exactly.

He went home, called Fred, checked that the jet was loaded properly and went to bed.

Tomorrow, paradise!

<u>*Moving In*</u>
**

CD and Alma were staying in a cabin just a little down the beach from Clint and Tyna that Clint and Nito had constructed for a guest house. Nick and Janet would arrive later. CD and Clint would go to Chiriqui Grande to meet Nick and Janet. CD would meet with the crew who were going to build the houses on the island. They were to start construction today. The early crew were coming into the beach when Clint and CD headed for Chiriqui Grande. Alma and Tyna were in Clint's smaller boat, on the way to the island.

It was a little drizzly at Chiriqui Grande, but was the kind of misty rain the people there ignored. After all, this was a coastal rain forest area!

CD went to the office of the aduana, where the building crew were waiting while the government people checked out the supplies that had been imported.

None. That went fast! They were headed for the island less than fifteen minutes later. Clint would wait for Nick and Janet at the bombas. He had his car to take whatever they brought to the boat.

Rojelio came to say Clint might be interested to know that two men and a woman had been asking a lot of questions about the Campbells. He refused them any information, saying it was an ongoing investigation. They made some statements intended to scare him into believing some bigshots from Panamá City would come and put him in his own cell if he didn't 'cooperate.'

"I was all innocence. I asked if they were threatening a police officer. They said they were warning a police officer. I said there was no legal difference. How would the lot of them like to spend ninety days in carcel?"

"To which they replied?"

"They just left."

"If they come back, or if anyone else asks too many questions, or if you are threatened in any little way, call me. You have my number. There's something very fishy going on here!"

"Fishing? I don't...?"

"An expression. It means 'very strange' in translation."

"Thank you, Clint. You are a friend. I will call you if there are further things to happen. I will certainly investigate the Campbell people as best I can."

"Take care, my friend."

"I will. Very cetainly."

Clint went on to the bombas. He was there for twenty minutes or so, talking with a number of people he knew. A busload of people on their way to Isla Colón stopped for snacks and the rest rooms. Clint told them about some of the places that would appeal to the different ages and interests.

The next bus was the one Janet and Nick were on. They loaded all their stuff into Clint's car, drove to the dock to transfer it into the boat, Clint took the car back to the friend's place where he kept it (the friend used it a lot. Clint, almost never, anymore.). They headed for Cusapín. Clint pointed to an island on the horizon, and said that was it.

"Do you mean that mountain?" Janet asked. "I had pictured a little island with a lot of coconut palm trees, like our place on Martinique!"

"It has plenty of that," Clint replied. "It also has bananas and pineapples and cashews and almonds and guanabana and oranges and lemons and avocadoes and mangos and mormones and jobitos and papayas and fifty others. Alma is going crazy. There are hundreds of varieties of orchids there. She found four types of vanilla, already, some with seed capsules ready to make vanilla flavoring. You saw from before how the real thing is a thousand times as flavorful as the crap in the states. We have fish and other seafoods of almost any type, as well as plenty of the natural food vegetables. I'll plant any that aren't already there. I think you could eat very well for six months and never have the same things twice in the time."

"We were here for two weeks before. We didn't have the same meal twice, then, except when we were in David, eating in the restaurants. I like the native foods, except that every meal has to have rice, which I ain't that overly fond of," Nick said. "In the restaurants, I could usually have potatoes, instead. I had to get used to not having bread with most meals.

"I did learn there were a lot of rice dishes that were damned good. Coconut rice is delicious. That rice pudding Alma made with coconut, pineapple, and raisins was fantastic, but she's got to be the best cook in the world! I like curry dishes with rice."

"You should have known Ben and Earl, on Isla Colón," Tyna said. She had just come from the house, where she had opened the guest room and readied it for them. "Earl was a cordon bleu chef and Ben was a natural cook. Together ... well!

"I have some things in the freezer. Conch, fish, crab, lobster, chicken, iguana, pork. You can fix whatever you like. We have to eat all that stuff before we move to the island. Clint will take the solar panels and storage, so we'll have everything about the same as here. Our one import from so-called civilized society. Electric stuff. There's TV and DVD and all that. We almost never use it. Clint uses the comp, sometimes. He's mostly retired from the detective thing. Only when it affects the comarca and our people, or when it's something he can't resist. He's a born detective. It's like that thing in one of Dave's books about a yak."

"I think I remember that. I read a lot of his books. Nick read a few," Janet said. "I liked that one. A Japanese man, talking about some of the people he was forced to do business with. 'You can take a yak from the fields, have it hand curried and petted by twelve beautiful virgins, feed it only the selected finest of grains, put it in a golden corral with the softest fine straw. It will remain a yak.' Something like that."

"I say you can take the animal out of the barn, but you can't take the barn out of the animal," Nick said. "If you're raised in a barn, you'll bray like a barn animal. Trite, but very true. It's all in how you was raised. Parents are pigs, you'll be a pig. In the work, I always admired anyone who could beat that fact. A few did. I saw several bigtime gangsters turn legitimate. I admired them for the strength it took to do that."

"Yeah. Greco and Donilleti. Mo Jefferson. I've heard of them. I had a friend who was as big (Marko Bocinni, who lived in Bocas as Manny Mathews. He raised a family he could be proud of), who turned one eighty. Pillar of the community. Pancho knows him. He calls Pancho Pancho (Anyone who called Pancho by his nickname, not "Mr. DeGulio, Sir!" was a close friend).

They talked for a long time. Janet and Nick moved in. Tyna and Janet were doing some things around the house, Nick and Clint went to the village for Nick's friends there to welcome him to the comarca.

It would be like that for about a month, then the island.

*

Nick and Janet met Clint at the bus stop and went to his place on the comarca in his boat. They moved into the guest house. The wives were doing something, getting ready to move to the island. He and Clint went to the village, where he remade his contacts with many of those fantastic people. He could fit here. That had worried him a lot. CD and Clint were millionaires – billionaires, in CD's case – but both preferred the lifestyle of the comarca.

He didn't think he could adjust to not having anything to do. Clint and CD were the same. Janet and Alma and Tyna were the same. He fully intended to become part of the comarca. He liked the responsible but easy lifestyle. He hoped he could become half as close to the Indios as Clint. He would have to get used to hugs whenever they met somewhere else or after he had been away for any length of time. They were a touching people.

They returned to the house after a couple of hours. CD was on the island. They would go out today. Jan and Tyna would go over tomorrow. Alma was hands-on about the construction, but not the bossy type. She would pitch in and help. Jan was like that.

Clint had some work to do around the place. He said it was small things that needed doing. Nick could do what he wanted.

Nick went to the beach to walk along. Two small boys and a girl came to walk with him. They didn't speak English, his Spanish was poor. He knew "Jontoro!" in the dialect meant welcome or good or something positive. It was a greeting as used by the Guayme, the neighboring Indios. "Coin" meant the same thing, and was used more by the Ngobe, though both used both terms.

These kids were seven or eight years old and were a kilometer away from home on a beach, alone. They were safer than any kids that age almost anywhere in the states. They knew more about life at that age than most in the USA at fifteen years. They lived with nature. They didn't fight it and didn't try to deny that they were human. The first time he and Janet were there, Nito, Clint's son, was telling about an older boy who had screwed him. Clint and Tyna were interested, he and Janet were shocked. Nito just said he didn't much care for it, but it wasn't so bad, either.

Clint saw how he was reacting, and said it happened to most people. Big deal! Why try to make the kid think he'd done anything wrong? Nito had consented. If he'd been raped, it would be a different thing. That, you take out on the one who did the raping, not on the victim.

He agreed, intellectually. Emotionally was a different thing.

Nito wasn't harmed by it in any way. He was as well-adjusted as most of the Indio kids, and was making a name for himself in police circles. Clint's daughter was making as much of a name for herself in medical.

He'd been back twice since that first trip. He saw that this society worked in ways the so-called "civilized" failed.

He chatted with the kids. They seemed to understand what he meant, even if they didn't know the words. He understood them. They did pick up a few English words. He learned that "dere" meant afternoon. When they parted, he said, "Jontoro dere!" They laughed and replied, "Coin dere!" The girl simply said, "Co!" He thought that was a shortened form of "Coin" they used as a reply. He went into the house. Janet and Tyna were cooking a large langosta for dinner. CD was back. Clint would be back when he got back. Nobody had a schedule.

He found he was sunburned. He'd forgotten he had been inside so much and walked for more than two hours on a beach in the full sunlight! Tyna used some aloe that was right by the door and had him eat four large carambolas. They are a very high quality source of vitamin C. The inflamation was gone in half an hour or so, and the soreness. He had a little tan from Florida, so it wasn't a severe burn. In the morning it was hardly noticeable.

Things went along like that for the next two days, then Clint said he had a case he was going to spend some time on. He had retired more than thirty times before, but something that intrigued him came along now and then.

"Two people were killed. Their car was pushed over the side of a mountain with them in it. I solved that in a day, but those two didn't exist a couple of years ago. Now some strange people are asking a lot of questions. I want to know what's behind it."

"When I came on that kind of thing it almost always turned out to be someone on witness protection."

"I have someone who can usually check that kind of thing fast. I don't think so."

"I can check with Pancho. He finds that kind of thing faster than anyone else I've encountered."

"I did. He can't find anything.

"Want a little diversion?"

"It could be interesting."

Clint used the computer to contact Manny Mathews, who was actually a retired mafia don from California Clint had helped to establish a new identity. He went legitimate, but had held onto his power. He couldn't find much. The Campbells could be Larry Holden and Marsha Peabody. They had disappeared at about the same time, two years ago. They had some kind of information the US military wanted or didn't want out or something. The only connection he could find between them was e-mails that seemed to be coded, but even that wasn't certain.

Clint thought. JK, who worked for CD for years, was a genius when it came to computers. He had developed a number of programs that decoded whatever needed decoding. He was on his own island in the Caribbean. Clint could call him, but it might be better if CD did.

He called to the island. CD used his special cellular phone with the coded and scrambled signal. JK would check and call back when he had anything. Send him a number.

JK could find almost anything about almost anyone if he had any kind of number that would be somewhere on the net. A Social Security or passport number was best, but even an old address or phone number could be traced easily. A drivers' license or fishing license, a license tag number – so long as it was a number that anyone would have registered for any reason with any government agency.

Clint had the passport numbers, but said they led to people who didn't exist a couple of years ago.

That wouldn't slow JK for one second! CD also gave him the names, Larry Holden and Marsha Peabody, and the information, uncertain, that they had something the military was interested in, though what that was about was a thing they could only guess at, at this point.

Nick strolled in with Janet. She said "Hi!" and went back toward their cabin. She was going with Alma and Tyna to Cusapín to help set up the materials for the new school year. Clint explained the case. Nick said he would like to try his hand at it. He knew from his trips before that the law was handled differently here than in Florida.

"We can each use our own methods. We share anything we learn. This isn't some kind of competition, unless or until something comes up that lets us have a little fun with it," Clint suggested. "We did have that one time we all worked on a case. It took us each the same time to solve it." (*Murder Divided by 3*)

"I'll use the secure comp in my plane with JK, first. He's the best bet we have to find who the Campbells were," CD decided. "If something military is involved, Crane's security clearances, particularly JK's, are for the top of the top secret crap."

"JK was a big help to us a few years ago, when that FBI man was murdered. That tied it to the Russian mafia. I was very damned glad Pancho is a friend, there!" (Nick Storie book 16: *Bad Move*)

"I think I can trace backward from something on a note to find who hired the killings," Clint said. "That will tell us if the military is behind it. I don't want the US military doing anything here in Panamá. They would work only through the CIA, and that leads inevitably to disaster."

For the time being, Nick would stay on the comarca, CD would go to David, where his jet was hangared, Clint would go to Isla Colón.

*

Nick walked along the beach in thought. He went to the

Page 27

computer and started bringing up past records of Larry Holden. All he knew about him from the information Clint supplied was that he was from Fresno, California, had worked for various companies having to do with home security. He had invented an infra-red movement detector that was popular. He was fairly wealthy from royalties.

The military had those things out the ying-yang. There had to be more.

He went to the patent description. From what little he knew, Nick thought it was a standard type of thing.

He traced the name through the patent offices. Holden had also patented a very small laser range finder. It had applications for construction. It was accurate to within four inches at one mile.

That could very well have military significance!

Okay. Just for a direction, he would concentrate on that.

Why would the military have him assassinated for that? It was patented. Anyone could get the manufacturing specs and build the thing, so long as Holden got royalties. Snipers and missiles and what have you could use it – so long as they considered other factors. A thirty mile an hour crosswind would possibly make the accuracy within four feet instead of four inches. Drop or rise, another consideration.

Also, Holden's invention would put him in it, not the woman. What was her connection?

Marsha Peabody. Born in Oregon, worked in Silicon Valley for a few years. Patented a laser-driven self-focusing microscope. A boon to electron microscopes that had a problem when the focus was off at one millionth of an inch. Her ultra-short focusing laser held focus at three ten-millionths of an inch.

That was all.

Would combining those two things give a better targeting ... no. Millionths of an inch had no application at a mile.

There had to be something. Nick was sure he had a part of an answer. Too bad he didn't really know what the question was!

**

Clint asked around. It was too bad he didn't have Judi Lum here to help him. There had been no one in the world more able in getting information.

From what he knew and suspected, his quarry would go to the Toro Loco and the Rip Tide. He or she would be the slightly obnoxious pushy type.

Santo Smith, an Indio friend, said it could be the Warren woman. Kind of brassy, but fun. From Texas. She went to the Toro Loco and to Gary's.

"She's easy to find. You're a gringo, so she'll call you Fred. I'm Indio, so she calls me Tonto. She calls the Latins Pedro and the blacks Sambo."

Anderson was black – but she might have assumed he was Latino.

At seven thirty, Clint went into the Toro Loco. He spotted Margarita Warren right away. She was at the bar, ordering drinks for everyone. There were six others beside Clint and her in the place. She announced she had bought all the guys a drink. That meant she was entitled to get in their pants. Isn't that the way men thought?

"You don't have to buy me a drink for that! I'm ready without it!" one man said quickly.

"And if I didn't get there first, you would have bought me a drink and figured you owned me for the night, right?" It was obviously a routine with her. The guys seemed to like her. This was a standing joke.

She noticed Clint. "New face! First dibs!" she cried.

"No problem. The gay guys aren't here until later," another fired back.

Page 29

"You don't prefer gay guys, do you? With my luck, you would."

Clint fell right into it. "Only on alternate Thursdays. This is Friday."

"You look like a gringo, but not like a gringo. What?"

"Ngobe. Call me Tonto."

Santo came in just before that. He said, "No! I'm Tonto! She can call you abuelo!"

She laughed. "I'm Rita. You are?"

"Clint. I'll call you Sally."

"Sally? If there's one thing I'm not, it's a Sally. You that famous dick?"

"He's the famous dick. Both kinds," Santo replied.

"She said dick. Not dickhead," John, a man Clint knew for years, said. Clint gave him the bird.

They had a good time, joking most of the three hours Clint spent there. She got him aside one time for a few minutes and asked if he was looking for her.

"No more. I already found you. Same process with you as with Anderson, or do you know who you're working for?"

"Cool! What gave me away?"

"Pedro. Aces."

She nodded, and grinned. "I don't know what it's about. I get a free vacation in heaven for it. Politics in it, but they were spies from Iran. They swore that."

"They were Americans from California and Oregon who had some information about some politicians."

She looked shocked. "You aren't shitting me, are you?"

"No."

"If I knew, I think I'd tell you. I'll damned well find out!"

"No! You'd be a spy they would hire someone else to get rid of! Just don't let anyone know you or I said anything except that this is a really open society where you can have fun. I'll handle it my own way."

"They really would. Deal, Sam Spade!"

The rest of the night went well. Clint had a few things he wanted to do in the morning, then would head back home.

***

"JK, I have to get some information on a couple of people who didn't exist two years ago. Military might be involved. Not WP." CD gave him what information he had. JK would get back.

CD had a lot of experience with the military methods. Crane manufactured various top secret devices. He wasn't able to get out of that end because of the past. Crane had been used through a lot of things, each of less worth than the last. It was sickening to know what governments had become. Greedy little people vying for money and position, then didn't know what to do with it when they had it. So they went after more.

He was glad to be away from that. His kids had it to deal with. He was sorry he couldn't divest and tell the whole world to kiss his ass.

JK sent the information as he found it. Nothing new. Both he and JK felt that knowing the connection with the two people would probably give them the answers they were after.

JK would trace back further. Maybe he could find where the two met. That could be the basis for what happened since that time.

CD got his helicopter and went to the island. The house would be ready for occupancy in another week. Alma was already designing and building her orchid jungle.

JK called to say he'd sent what might mean a lot. It was from before either of them had invented anything. It would be in scrambled code at the jet. He even told CD that in a code they had worked out. It sounded like he was asking about the construction of the house.

CD got back to the chopper and headed for David.

The code light was on. That was a sign that JK's little invention that found listeners had found listeners. What they wouldn't know was that the two of them would chat about things at the Crane plant while a totally separate system downloaded what they were really finding.

Just to be mean, CD discussed a top secret laser device they were developing for the space program, such as it was at the moment. He was sure no one listening had authorization to hear a word of it. The real part was in a special code it would take eight months to decipher – if they could find the base, at all. When it was all there, JK said he had a project he was studying to make light turn back on itself.

The governments who knew of JK would go crazy trying to figure how that could be done. They knew that, if JK Kiley said it would work, it would work.

The coded way he said it was that you did that every time you looked in a mirror, but the "DUH!-geniuses" in the military would never think of something so obvious. Maybe ten million of their budget would go to try to find a way to turn light back on itself.

CD giggled and went to the downloaded files. They seemed to be videos.

First was Marsha Peabody behind a podium. CD listened as she expounded on inserting a reader in a focusing unit that used a Dopler effect program to give an exact distance as close as a ten millionths of an inch at one inch or one half inch at one mile.

It seemed there was a way ... maybe that was the principle of Holden's invention.

There were flashes of two other people giving speeches, then Holden. This was where they first met. This was where two ideas combined to ... what?

He watched three more videos, only one of which Holden appeared in.

It seemed to be extensions of what the first had been. She had come up with a device that used the Dopler effect to find things that ... so that was it! A combination of Holden's device and hers would make it possible, even probable, that you could hit a target within half an inch of dead center at three miles distance!

Was that a military motive or not? Dead-accurate snipers at three miles was getting pretty well up there.

Why would they kill the two inventors? What was he missing?

*

Nick sat back to think. He had found a thing or two. The two dead people had made speeches at the same seminaries. All that was public property. Shutting them up made no difference to anything he could see.

He soon called Clint to discuss what was known, so far. Clint conferenced CD into it. CD and he were doing the "what?" part while Clint did the "who?" part. It seemed that Holden and Peabody had come up with a device that could have pinpoint accuracy at three miles and that, seeing how screwed up it already seemed, the CIA was likely to be behind the assassinations. After the chat, Nick went back to the computer, but couldn't think of anything to check. It would be tangental. JK would probably be the one to find anything.

Maybe.

Why were they in Panamá? Was it just a coincidence – or were they here for a specific reason?

Another thing to think about. Did they communicate ... they would have had to. They communicated in a way that someone was able to tap into. That they had invented something else was a likely scenario.

He used the special phone JK had given him several years ago that he used about four times per year to keep up to date with him. JK said he had fiddled with the idea a bit. Maybe he could find a tidbit or two. He had the e-mails and blogs the two had used. Some kind of rough system was used to scramble a lot of it up, but that kind of thing was patterned. He could get around most of it.

They chatted about the island. JK would like to visit.

When they rang off, Nick sat back to think. A few minutes

later JK started sending him the e-mails he could use.

He had another idea and asked that JK send a list of all e-mail addresses either received or sent to. He soon had several hundred addresses, and correlated them.

He felt he had someting useful in that, but couldn't think of what.

He scrolled down the lists on split screen. Both sent things to two addresses that never responded in any way.

What was that about? If they sent something to an address a couple of times and got no response they would probably not send anything else.

He saw the spiral arrow on every one of those messages. He was about to ask JK what it meant, then remembered seeing the arrows on his own e-mail. It meant the message was forwarded to that address.

He checked the sources of the forwarded messages. They were all scientific research papers.

He called JK. He asked if it was possible the addresses were storage areas. JK started to ask what he was talking about, but said, "So. They each have a site they use to store and study the newest ideas and theories. They didn't directly communicate through their regular e-mails, but I'll bet a billion those two sites communicated!"

"Would the CIA or whatever figure that out?"

"Huh! Only if somebody drew them a diagram! I'll see what I can find at those two addresses. I'll get back to you. Is CD in on it?"

"Yeah, JK. Him and Clint."

**

Rita Warren was out of it, past being the block point if anyone came this far. That meant concentrating on the three people who had tried to intimidate Rojelio. This was a disconnected mess. Nick or CD might come up with something to form at least a basic link.

Clint went back to Chiriqui Grande to talk with Rojelio. He got the information collected. Rojelio had the sense to get his information in ways they wouldn't know. Nito had shown him how to check for passport numbers and such at hotels and for use of credit cards and license numbers, among others.

Irene Mary Smith, from Baltimore, Maryland. Tourist. Used Master Card in name of Jefferson Lincoln Company, billed through KFSC Diversified, Orlando, Florida. He couldn't find much about the company. Small manufacturer of specialized application connectors. What the hell did that mean?

She was a fashion designer.

Thomas Allen Jones, Houston, Texas. Tourist. Used Visa Card in name of StartlersStarters, Inc. A small company that produced starters for flourescent lights. He was a carpenter.

Robert William Brothers, Atlanta, Georgia. Tourist. Used Visa Card in name of Jefferson Applicators. Another small company that didn't seem to do anything. He was a used car salesman.

Let's see. Three people with common names who used credit cards from companies they didn't work for. That smelled strongly of CIA. A fashion designer, a carpenter, and a used car salesman acting like big bad govmint agents y'all, asking about murdered inventors of things with military applications.

KFSC. Kentucky Fried Space Chicken?

He checked the company. There was a little less than nothing about it available. Dr. Alexander Fieldinghouse was, apparently, chairman and CEO.

He checked on Fieldinghouse. He was a specialist in mineral deprivation on the cellular level for NASA.

He might well work with electron microscopes, but so what?

Nothing even that interesting in the others.

Either there was a connection with NASA – no! It was set up to make people who investigated think that! If there was one sure thing, this wasn't directly linked to NASA. If it was there would be no such item to catch the eye. It was too far for it to be CIA. This was all crap that was designed to keep anyone from finding anything.

Okay. Something that would strike within a half inch in three miles of very difficult trajectory. A sniper's tool.

What about at a hundred miles?

He sat back to study some papers, but there didn't seem to be that much more. He was still at square one.

He decided to see if he could accidentally run into the three. Rojelio said they were staying at the hotel, last night. They had gone somewhere in the morning and would be back later in the afternoon, according to Luis, at the hotel desk.

Clint went into the restaurant to sit at a table next to three gringos to order the carne corriente. The three seemed very interested in him, so he smiled and asked if he had done anything to draw attention to himself. Irene answered, "Aren't you Clint Faraday?"

"So I'm told."

"You were a close friend of that Dave character, who invented some kind of super weapon the Indios used?"

"Dave? Yes."

"Did you ever see the weapon?"

"They tell me I did. I didn't know that's what it was. I can't tell you much of anything about it, except it looks like something very ordinary." (Clint Faraday book 19: *A Moving Target*)

"We went to Cusapín. We talked with your wife. She said she'd heard about it, but didn't have time for such things. Those two gringas with her said they knew Dave from Florida, but didn't know anything about any super weapon.

One is ... I guess you would know. They were at the place Grimes is building. Grimes owns Crane, who produce weapons for the US military."

"Alma? Janet and Tyna. None of them ever interfere with the husbands' work. They're individuals with their own interests, one of which is definitely *not* weapons. Dave was more about the orchids with them."

"I'm Bob Brothers. The Indios shot down planes at three kilometers? How could they get such an accurate aim? I hear the holes they had in them were the size of a nickel!"

"I really don't know. Dave explained once to that Leventhal person. I heard it. It was about time and a velocity of sixty or seventy thousand miles per hour, so there weren't any detectable, what did he say? Perturbations? Something about time ... something. Dilatation in a contained volume? Something."

Clint would have a little fun with them. He did know a little about the weapon. Dave used some arguments about it that he said were pure bullshit, but the donkey/carrot military scientists would fall for it.

"Gheee? Seventy thousand miles per hour? That would vaporize whatever he was shooting!" the one Clint assumed was Tom Jones cried.

"Marbles. He said that wouldn't matter, because it would be halfway to the moon before the molecules had time to separate or something. Once out of the atmosphere, it would all coalesce."

"Marbles? What...?" Irene asked.

"He once picked up a child's marble on the road and said it was hard to believe a ten year old could build something with things found in a garbage dump that would shoot an object like that through the hardest armor we made. It could shoot down the stealth bomber. It was silent. I don't remember much. It wasn't something I could get intersted in, unless it was used as a murder weapon. Military? Who gives a happy shit?"

"But ... how does it work?"

"I don't have a tiny little clue. Something about eddy currents and vibrations and time distortion."

"A glass marble? You can't produce eddy currents in glass!" Jones cried.

"No, I can't. He could, I suppose. The thing did work.

"Ah, here's my repast. Excuse me. Have a good evening."

The rest of the time he was there the three were arguing about marbles and glass and eddy currents. They wanted to ask Clint what he meant about time, but it was too plain he didn't want to be disturbed while he ate. When he finished, he stood, nodded at them, and walked out before they could question him again.

He went to the boat and contacted CD and Nick to tell him the latest. It was about aiming Dave's weapon.

"But they don't have any such weapon," CD pointed out. "JK talked about it with Dave. He says it's what Dave claimed, so far as he could discover. It would as much as destroy civilization if it got out. A ten year old could build it, and it would shoot down the stealth bomber – and more. If you knew any nutcase or terrorist or whatever could build one and shoot you down, would you get on a plane?"

"Sort of the same he told us. One person could cut off a highway or hole a gas line or generator or whatever. It works because of something in his theory of the omniverse.

"If JK says it works, it's sort of scary."

"I've heard you like understatement."

They chatted a minute, then rang off. Was this a case of some organization adding one and one and getting seven point five four? Was even the CIA that stupid?

To Clint, it looked a bit too much for CIA. They definitely weren't involved. They fucked up things after they got into them and while getting into them. This was making it seem like the idiot phase was before. *Not* their style.

***

CD took the laptop from the chopper into the cabin and put it onto the table in the kitchen. He took the BugChaser from the bag of groceries (it was disguised as a gas sparker/starter) and glanced at the tell-tale as he laid it on the stove. There was an electronic device in the room.

He put a pan of water on the stove and used the starter to ignite the gas. It didn't take the first flick. He flicked it again.

The device was under the edge of the shelf. He laid the sparker almost on top of it and called to ask if Alma was close. He knew she was at the island. Calling made the BugChaser note that the bug was video and audio. One circuit sound-accessed, the other motion accessed.

He put a spoonful of instant coffee in a cup and poured the hot water over it (which should be a dead giveaway, if they knew anything at all about him. He drank only the special mix of coffee Alma made). He added a spoon of sugar, then sat at the table to take his cell phone out of its case and make a call (that was to a recorder on his jet). The call would go out scrambled and coded. They would feel they had what they needed from what he said.

He acted like he was making a report to JK. He said he had determined that the people in question were operatives, but not from NASA, FBI, CIA, or Pentagon. That meant they were agents for someone else. The last thing the US, even the military, wanted was for the inventors of such a thing killed. It was low possibility that there could be any defense against the item in focus, but they would be that low possibility. Only JK, in his experience with such things – and he had a *lot* of experience through Crane – could possibly find a defense.

Who would want ... he stopped. Who, indeed?

He sent the code for JK to actually read what he was sending. He might have stumbled on something.

The light came on that said JK was listening.

"JK, someone has been threatened with that weapon. It's stronger than when Dave said he would put instructions on the web and other places if certain practices weren't stopped."

"It's likely. Dave made his threat against corrupt politicians, but the money people got the message. If such a thing were to be released, they know damned well they would be the first targets. The world's become a slavehold for those people, and everyone knows it. It's why you're smart to be on that comarca. The crumble of the money world won't affect the Indios. I can't see ... I'll be damned. So that's what it is! It's everything Dave said it was. It's something the militaries of every advanced country on Earth have been doing research on. He found a way to make it work! I'll be damned!"

"What?"

"I know what Dave's weapon is. I'll make one this afternoon to test. It really is something simple beyond your ability to believe. This is rich!"

He caught himself. He realized CD wouldn't be doing this for any reason except to throw off listeners. He might have said too much, but he would try to fix that. He remembered how Clint reported that he snowed them with BS.

"CD, every country on this planet has been working on a laser-driven fusion reactor. We've all had a little success. It's a matter of a *sustained* reactor. Dave's zero theory says that only time and motion exist. He pounded on that fact hundreds of times. That's what the gyroscope experiments were about.

"I'll be damned! He was right about wrapping yourself in a different time volume. It's so damned easy to do, particularly when your volume is less than a cubic foot."

CD caught on. This had nothing to do with the weapon, it was to get them looking in all the wrong places.

"I follow a little. Explain."

"A gyroscope seems to affect time along Einsteinian lines. The omniverse is time and motion in fixed equation. Increase one, and you decrease the other to the exact same balance, but mirror. Increase time, decrease motion. Decrease motion, increase time.

"The thing simply emplaces an eddy in time in any object whatever. It increases time. You place the object in that frame and move it in a direction, always a straight line, by inertial laws. You increase motion within that frame, then revert instantly back to what we consider normal. The object increases its motion directly in this frame as time drops to ratio. C squared, remember, so you get a logarythmic function on the base determiner of inertia.

"What happens, you move an object at fifty miles per hour in a time frame a reverse multiple of what we call 'here' in this frame. Suddenly remove the barrier, so to speak. The object is suddenly moving at the multiple in this frame. It's Einsteinian, and in balance. The object you were moving at fifty miles per hour in that frame is now moving at a hundred thousand miles per hour in this frame. Not that much. Cubed for ... scale fourth log ... eighty seven thousand miles per hour. Whatever. I have an idea."

JK was known to get an idea and simply walk away like the rest of the world didn't exist. CD knew this was to scare the holy living piss out of whoever was behind this mess. It was pure crap from the get-go. They would know JK was a genius without equal. They'd probably work for hours to find what a logarythmic function on a base determiner of inertia was.

Now. See what fish strikes at that lure!

Nick and friends were looking over the house on the island. It was going faster than CD or Nick could believe. They expected delays and additions and permits and bureaucracy. Clint knew he was respected by what few such agencies had involvement. The Indios building the house would work on this as if it were Clint working with them on a project for the comarca. Nick and CD and wives were getting used to the hugs every time they met any of the people from the comarca. The kids were working as much as their fathers. The younger ones doing the lighter work. Two of the girls, maybe eight or nine years old, were keeping food available. They were already good cooks.

The boys between six and ten were making garden plots or working on Alma's orchid gardens.

It was near noon, so everyone stripped and went into the river that ran a few hundred meters from the house to cool off and clean up. Nick, Janet, CD, and Alma seemed uncertain, then stripped and joined them. The men wrestled and dunked each other. They played and laughed a lot.

Clint saw Janet sitting on a large flat rock, crying. He asked why.

"This is beautiful."

"What?"

"Life. All of it."

He nodded. They all climbed onto the rocks to sit for a few minutes to dry off, put on their clothes, and went to the meal. This one was a sort of seafood stew. It was a little like paella. Mussels, lobster, crab, fish, conch, shrimp, octopus, in a brown sauce, served over rice. It had a slightly curry flavor. There was a pasta salad with pineapple, banana, coconut, and flakes of jobito, with a dressing not unlike mayonaise.

Guanaba chicha and/or coffee.

"My God!" Janet exclaimed. "I've eaten in some of the best restaurants! These kids could put them out of business in a week!

"Oh, Nick! When we were married you promised me the stars and planets! This is so much more!

"Clint, what is this?"

She was holding up a small piece of fruit from the salad.

"Jobito. Smell it."

She did. "Sort of like ... fruit punch?"

"And it tastes like fruit punch."

After the meal, Nick, CD, and Clint helped carry the heavy nispero for the house. It is a wood that is as heavy as steel and about as strong. Clint had bought special corundum drills for the construction. A regular nail, unless the wood was drilled, would just bend. Concrete nails would penetrate, but would tend to split the wood. It did not deteriorate. It was too hard for termites or bacteria or fungus to affect.

Alma said the red wood was beautiful. She would like to carve some things in it, but didn't have good enough tools. Janet had some tools she used to carve jade. They would both make things.

They went back to Cusapín late in the afternoon. Renaldo said there were three people who had come before, and a fourth. They were at the hospidaje. Did Clint want to talk with them or wait until tomorrow?

"I'm off duty today. Tomorrow."

They went to his house. CD got Nick and Clint aside and told them about the bugs. Nick shook his head sadly and looked a little irritated. Clint said he knew. He was going to warn them. He had his own recorders on since this case started. They told about what they had learned and about JK's involvement.

"I can picture their scientists sitting around roaring at each other about logarythmic functions and eddy currents!" Nick said.

"When I said seventy thousand miles per hour, that Bob Bill Brothers character pissed in his pants," Clint said. "I told JK about that. It's where he came up with his figure.

"I still want to know what it's about. They can kill each other off or whatever. I don't care. I don't want them on the comarca. I won't put up with them dragging anyone else into it."

"I want to know who's behind it," Nick replied. "They already had two people killed. We have to get it through to them that was a mistake that never should have been made."

"We have to find why they were killed. None of this will make any sense until we know that."

"Why they were here is more important, I think," Clint warned. "Dave's dead and gone. There's nothing he left that they could be after, unless they think he left one of us or one of the Indios with something.

"He did, but not this end of the comarca."

"Maybe that's it. Maybe they only know the thing was used on the comarca, and that he spent so much of his time here," Nick suggested. "I would think we could distract them to another part of the comarca where there isn't anything to grab some time to find who's behind it."

Clint grinned. "Buabidi and Soloy. The museum. We might just accidentally let it slip that Dave said he had put something in the museum archives to be found when directed or when something specific happened.

"Let's go back to the house. I'm tired. Tomorrow might be a fun day, but be careful. Try to get it away from here. The women aren't any part of it. Get them involved, and I'll eliminate them as a problem, myself. Permanently."

They agreed with that.

**

The morning was spectacular. Sunrises are as colorful as sunsets here. The women were going to help in the puebla for awhile, then go to the island. Nick would hitch a ride with CD on the chopper to David. He would check on some ideas there and buy some more practical clothes. What he had was okay in town, but not where he would spend most of his time. CD had to make some arrangements about things in Florida. Clint would do some things around the place and get ready to move to the island. They would all be back by nightfall, or would call if they wouldn't get back until tomorrow.

Tomorrow, Clint would go to Buabidi, then return through Soloy. He had innocently made a remark about Dave leaving something at the museum he wanted to study to Tyna last night, while standing two feet from one of their bugs.

There was a three day waiting list for anyone to get into the museum. Clint was Ngobe. The Ngobe could go in anytime they liked. After all, it was *their* museum! (Clint Faraday, book 51: *Dead Man Talking*)

Everyone left, except Clint. He went through a lot of things and was setting up the water line to the shower at the palmfrond hut by the beach when four people came strolling casually along. It was Irene and friends, and another man. They waved and called and came over. The third man was introduced as Gordon Jones, a friend who just *happened* to be spending a month on Isla Colón, and had run into them in Chiriqui Grande.

"Uh-huh. Too much like Key West for my tastes. Another tourist trap in the Caribbean. Whoopee!" Clint replied. "Kind of like the comarca? I would think you were more city-attuned."

"It's beautiful here. Peaceful. I still like more the expensive hotel route," Jones said. "I'm spoiled and lazy, and know it." He had a sort of strange accent. He was darker than the other three, but not quite the Latino dark.

"Europe? Your accent?" Clint replied.

"I don't have an accent. All of you do," he replied, with a laugh. "Belgium."

"I'm the type who thinks a tent is good enough. I'm just getting too old to live like that anymore. Basic house is fine."

"Yes. You are worth several tens of millions of dollars, but prefer a simple life. I can't understand that, but each to his own.

"You met that scientist who had the age treatment thing (Clint Faraday, book 54: *Death From Natural Causes*). Are you using it? I know you are in your late seventies, yet you appear to be perhaps fifty five."

"No way! JK is using it, but just so long as he can be productive. He's fifty something and looks like maybe thirty."

"I heard about that, but don't quite believe it. Is that doctor really a hundred years old?"

"A hundred forty or so. Yes."

"Why didn't this Dave character use it? He was doing a lot of things that needed finishing." He seemed to know immediately he shouldn't have mentioned Dave. He colored. "So. Now you know this isn't a chance encounter."

"Never thought it was."

"It's about that weapon. It has a lot of people almost terrified. The evidence is that it is what he said. If it were to be described it could disrupt modern society somewhat."

"Ah! So you like understatement, too! It would destroy modern society, if what I'm told is true. The very last thing you or anyone else should be doing is trying to find what it is. From what Dave told me, too many people would know what it was if they saw it, but I saw it and didn't know it.

"It wouldn't affect us here. It would be unbelieveable what would happen if it was in the hands of most people. Just the part that no plane would dare to ever leave a runway would put civilization into a tailspin that it might not be able to survive. The fact a few people could cut off the food and water and fuel from the cities is, to use a little understatement, myself, chilling. Add that power could be stopped by a nutcase or two.

"I'd estimate more than half the population of the Earth would be dead within three months. After it starts, the big money people who have used and manipulated the world more and more would all be fertilizer. Not one politician would survive more than a week. Most bureaucrats would be among the late.

"Yet you come here to try to find it? Have you considered that there's no defense?"

"We're looking for what it is so we can develop a defense!"

"Listen closely. This is something Dave and *JK Kiley* said. Now concentrate.

"*There is no defense.* You could nuke any area where it was known, but that would be the entire planet."

"No. It is a device that operates on inertial principles of velocity. There are ways."

"At a few thousand miles per hour, maybe. JK said a little piece of balsa wood traveling at those velocities would penetrate the best armor.

"One other little thing to consider, then we can drop this stupid conversation.

"A bit of nuclear material (he would scare them a bit more with something JK said, as reported by CD) being struck with almost anything at that velocity would compress to critical in a pico-second. Think about it.

"How's the weather in Belgium this time of year?"

"So! That's what was meant by the laser fusion process that, uh, that, um, Dr. Flowers was talking about."

"It's been a bit hot here. Good thing we have the ocean breeze. Not unpleasant at all."

"Point taken. We still have to try."

"Leave the people here out of it. Mess with any of my friends or the comarca and you're crab bait – if you're lucky. Killing the two people who could most likely find some kind of way to help you was stupid beyond belief."

"Which shows you know half of what you think you know. That was done to stop the device being placed into the wrong hands."

"Explain. Maybe I can find a little sympathy for you. They would have to have the device to be able to place it in anyone's hands."

"They had it. They were going to blackmail every government in the world. They wanted to rule the world!"

"What makes you think they had it?"

"They showed pictures of it being used on three plates of one inch armored steel. It penetrated. The scientists said there was no expansion. It had to be what they said."

"Show me the pictures. Also, show me any kind of proof of the penetration thing."

"Come with me to the hotel. I'll use the computer there to have my assistant send everything."

"As you know, I have everything you need in computers. Come on inside."

Jones turned to the other three, who had been just standing there through this. He told them to go to the hotel, then followed Clint inside. Clint turned on the computer.

There had been one demonstration of the thing, and that only to the Indios on the comarca. They had used three plates of armored steel.

Jones brought up a coded website and told the assistant to send all the material in file "dmsdy." It would come in coded, but Jones had a memory stick with the decoding program.

It was soon on the computer. Jones took out a memory stick and plugged it into the USB port. He opened the program, which was the demonstration on the comarca. There was then a video with an older man called Dr. Franken, who inspected the plates shown in the comarca video. He used very exact calipers and instruments, then decalred it was as represented.

The weapon was never shown on the comarca videos. Now, a shot of who Clint thought might be Peabody holding a thing that looked like something from the X-Files stockroom. Clint giggled.

"What?"

"The video was made on the comarca, except for the last part. How they got it, I have to find out. It's a true video, but nothing they had anything to do with.

"Does that silly thing Peabody's holding look anything at all like something that's common around the house that a ten year old kid could put together in two hours?"

"You mean they were going to try to blackmail all the major governments of the world with a bluff?"

"If you say so. It does explain why they were here. They had to go to the comarca and to one of two people to get that video. One or both are going to have to explain something that can't be explained. That ain't so easy to get away with on the comarca.

"Do you realize that this could have caused the information Dave left to be released? That it would bring about exactly the thing you were trying to avoid?"

"So. I can just ... so!

"Mr. Faraday, there will be no further interference here. We wish to avoid, at any cost, what could have happened."

Clint nodded. He left.

Clint called CD. He said he needed a helicopter ride across the comarca. He had most of the answers – if he could believe them. He sort of felt he could.

CD went to the jet to spend two hours on the things JK sent. This was the first time in many years JK didn't come up with answers to many things. He said Peabody, in particular, and Holden, to an extent, were egocentrist and introverted, at the same time. They were brilliant in a directed way, while not having a very firm grip on reality. Peabody was the type who might threaten the wrong people with something. Maybe she thought she could get her hands on Dave's weapon and blackmail the banks for a few billion or something. Holden would follow her.

"It leaves us with the possibility she actually did try to blackmail the wrong person or persons, huh?"

"I sort of think that may be behind it, CD. It's more than a little scary that she might have found the principle behind the thing. It's simple enough. The danger is that it would soon get out and people would find it, or try to. They would tend to study what she and Holden were doing and connect it.

There isn't much connection. Only the aiming part. With what it is, that isn't necessary."

"You know what it is?"

"Sure. Dave showed it to me twenty years ago. I made one a little more advanced than his."

"There really is no defense?"

"Not in any practical sense.

"CD, no agency set them up in a WP deal or anything else. They were doing it on their own. Holden knew enough to be able to do it better than the FBI or whatever. That leaves us with those clowns who killed them and what they're trying to accomplish. They represent something or somebody. I can't find who or what.

"CD, there's one person in this world I think could get to the bottom of this. Have Nick contact Pancho. I would, but Nick's the one he would trust over almost anybody."

"He already did. Pancho doesn't know what's going on.. Maybe he can be convinced to search out something. I have to agree he's the key to us ever learning much about this."

"Big money's behind it, somehow. I get that from the questions that aren't answered. About when the subject is suddenly changed. It becomes obvious pretty fast."

"Dave said all along that the first to go if the thing gets out will be the money manipulators who've held the world in economic slavery for most of recent history. Next would be politicians and bureaucrats, then anyone who had anyone else pissed at them."

"Be glad you're on that comarca. I'm damned glad I'm on this island. The one possible defense is the weapon, itself. You could get me at five miles range, but I could make damned sure no one nor anything got within five miles of here – by using the thing first. I don't see anyone getting on the comarca to attack you, but you have to never forget the entire Caribbean is open for someone to come in a boat. I'm more than twenty five miles from anything on these islands. No routes or anything else. You don't have that protection."

"If it comes to that I can be on the side where I'm building, anyway. They would have to go between this island and the comarca, and I can protect that – with the weapon."

"I'll make a couple and have them ready to deliver if it gets to that point."

CD knew that JK wouldn't take the chance of having CD or anyone else know what the thing was. He was all too familiar with what could be done to get the information from almost anyone.

"It's coming, isn't it, JK?"

"Eventually. We can hope some things will change before that happens."

"You can't know how glad I am that you're who you are."

"And vice versa."

*

Nick sat back to think for a minute.

There was something that made this a far different thing than it appeared. Something had happened that left him with a suspicion that the person or people behind a lot of this were *not* the ones they had been looking at.

He called Pancho. They discussed what was known. Pancho agreed that, if this was something set up or being used by any government or military agency on the Earth, JK would already know all about it. If it was from some mad scientist angle, JK would know. Peabody and Holden were that, but they were dead because whatever they planned had failed.

If it was anything from the underside of the equation, the mobs and dictators and such, Pancho would know. He would know if it was from political intrigues or whatever.

"Nickie, I think we have ... Nickie, let me check something. I will call again in a few minutes. Someone is manipulating all of the above. It could only be one thing. It could be the one thing that makes the above even exist."

"Greed. I know that, but ... I see. I'll wait for your call."

"Nickie, I'm going to take my family to JK's place. You and CD convince your own family to come with me. We can try to stop this, but it will be dangerous beyond any of our experiences. CD is among the wealthy, but his pitiful billions are nothing to these people. He was never in their select circle. If he had been, he would be in full control of Crane and would have several trillion dollars, not just a hundred billion. No one would know anything about him. The way it's set up, he would appear to have a couple of million and to live well, but the rest would be hiddden.

"Call CD and Clint together. I will call in exactly one hour."

Nick rang off, thought for a minute, then called Clint and CD. They would be on the island in one hour.

Page 53

Clint and Nick got out of Clint's boat at the little dock down from the house. CD came to greet them and ask what was going on. Nick explained that Pancho would call in about fifteen minutes. He had found who was behind the killings, if not why. He suspected Peabody and Holden were trying to terrorize the banks into giving them a few million dollars or something.

"They were trying to blackmail every government on Earth to become dictators," Clint replied. He explained what he'd learned.

"That fits with what Pancho thinks. Pancho is taking his family to JK's. He wants you two to get your families to go with him. JK has the weapon. He's going to make a couple to get to us if this happens. The one defense from the weapon is the weapon. It will be a local and temporary defense. We can defend here, and JK can defend his islands. The comarca won't be much affected, the cities are death traps that very few can escape.

"This is like a horror show, but it's very real."

"A fantasy horror show. We're living in it. If I'm dreaming, please! God that I don't believe in! Wake me up!" Nick cried.

Pancho called. Everything would be in place and ready. He was safe enough for the moment, but they had to be ready. They would have ten minutes to move if it came about.

"... and Clint. You asked, several times, why so many weird things with international importance happened in Panamá. Do you see, now?"

Clint paused. "Yeah, Pancho. Because one or more of those people are right here. The question is, who? Can we root them out and get them out of here?"

"Yes. We must root them out. They are not reptilian or any

of that silliness, except in their thought patterns. They have made themselves a breed apart. I think their part of evolution is about past.

"You will say we must warn them or something. I say, 'Why would you want to?'

"I will investigate, in my way, with what methods and tools are at my disposal. All of you do the same.

"These people have caused wars and worse. Think of them as mass murderers on the order of and worse than Hitler, Pol Pot, and Stalin combined.

"I am serious about this."

They had to agree with that.

*

Nick walked slowly along the beach. This was paradise.

Why here? Why now? When everything was falling into place to where he could find some peace and contentment, why did it have to suddenly cave in like this?

He had lived a charmed life, and knew it. He had often said he had to be the luckiest one slob in the world.

He was here. It was the place all this crap would affect least. His luck was running on full tilt. The same was true of CD and Clint. CD had always had an easy life, in most ways. Clint had started a hard life that had turned into a fantastic one.

All of them took danger to others as a personal affront when it came from the sleazebags of the world. All of them had very strong senses of right and wrong. They agreed on most points. They were also, after life's lessons, pragmatic to a degree they hadn't been in earlier life.

His son and daughter had been convinced to take a month's vacation with Pancho and family on JK's islands. CD's family and Tony Jacobi's family from Florida were going.

It wouldn't be possible to take along a lot of friends. A place where one had to be practical. JK was practical. He said who could or could not come.

This was peace and tranquility on the surface. Him on this beach, with the palms and fleecy clouds, the surf rolling in.

Underneath, it wasn't close to that.

**

Clint got off the chopper in Buabidi and went to the council building. Naldo and Elena greeted him. He said he was there on a serious matter. A breach of faith by one or both of two people.

"Who has charge of the records of the time when the company was trying to make an open-pit phosphate mine in the comarca? The time when the weapon was used?"

Elena looked thougthtful, then went to the files to check.

"Wilam Flores ... no, he died just three months ago. Gloria Comacho."

"I have some serious ... died? How?"

She got another file from another cabinet. "He died from a drug overdose."

"He what?!"

"Dios mio!" Naldo cried. "He did not use drugs! He would not be permitted to have access to any of this, if he did!"

Clint stared at the wall for a few seconds. "Do you have records of the people here for the museum at that times? Will there be records of anyone who came to speak with him?"

"Of course," Elena answered. "We use the system in the offices you had installed. Everything is on memory sticks. Even videos."

"I'll need for three days before he died. Maybe longer, but that should have it."

She went to a rack with thousands of small cubbies to look at the dates on each in a section marked "Consultants – Wilam Flores" to hand Clint three memory sticks. She pointed to a computer in a small cubicle. He went to boot up and insert the first.

There was a list of names and times. None seemed to be in any way familiar.

The second had Dr. Karl Franken, Elsa Jones, and Daniel Helper. - 3:30PM.

He brought up the time on the memory stick. Peabody, Holden, and the Dr. Franken on the other video.

They discussed the museum a moment, then Franken produced a paper to hand to Wilam, who looked at it and inserted it into a reader, which showed. It was a request to be allowed to inspect the artifacts from the time for a scientific analysis. Flores said he must meet with the council. He felt there would be no problem, so long as the weapon itself was not discussed in any way.

They were to return tomorrow at nine for the answer.

Clint sat back. So the analysis was legitimate. What Peabody and company probably didn't know was that Wilam didn't know anything at all about the weapon.

He put in the next memory strip. 9:00. They were waiting in the office. Wilam came in and said Dr. Franken was granted one half hour to study the materials. He gave them the copy of the comarca video. Peabody and Holden could not attend.

The next morning Wilam was found in his house, dead of an overdose of drugs. Several. Scopolamine was one of them.

So. They followed him home and drugged him, but he didn't know diddly-shit about the weapon. Clint thought. *They were now murderers. I have to find Franken to know if he was part of that.*

He went back to the second stick and brought up the request, It was from a scientific committee in Panamá City. It was signed by Emilio Bouher, recording secretary. Physical Science Advisory Committee International.

They were safe, to that point. No one had the weapon now,

except JK. He called JK and told him what had happened and what he expected.

Then he headed for Panamá City.

***

JK called CD and told him what Clint reported. He suggested that CD and Nick find where Franken was staying while Clint investigated that coommittee. There were a few records of such a committee, but it was a little nothing thing, so far as he could find. It was all too possible it was something set up for future use, when and if needed.

CD agreed. He could get cooperation from immigration, because Clint had vouched for him. Clint had enough to do to try to find what was behind the whole thing. He suspected he knew.

"Uh-huh," JK replied. "It's exactly what I suspected from the first. Peabody was a total fool to try to pull that bluff. I can't understand why she would do anything that stupid."

"You know something? Franken was sent by that committee."

There was a short silence. "So Franken was sent to learn if there was an authentic danger. He determined there was. He didn't know they didn't get any information about the weapon, whatever. Peabody's mistake was in letting her ego make her think she was in control. She didn't have any insurance. Exit the lovely lady."

"She thought Holden would be her insurance. That would have worked ten percent of the time if they weren't together. They were able to take her out and cancel the policy at the same time."

"And it would have worked if Holden were somewhere he couldn't be found – until he was found."

"But you *do* have the weapon. We'll have to use that."

Page 58

*

Nick considered something. He wondered if Clint and CD had come to the same conclusions. The bluff was exactly that. That she didn't have the weapon was shown when that video was taken with her holding a silly movie prop. If seeing the weapon would show people what it was, no such video would exist. There would have been a video of her using the weapon, but the weapon wouldn't be shown. This was, as in one of Dave's books, an ocean liner in a puddle.

He considered things. It still left a huge problem for the world. That same bunch of throwbacks was in charge. Maybe a way to pry a little of their control from them could come from it.

That would occur to CD and Clint.

And to JK.

He turned back. He would go out to the island and help with the house and gardens. He liked working with these people. They were real and basic.

He was going to find contentment here – and more.

**

Clint got off the chopper and headed for the address the police had given him for the home of Emilio Bouher. It was in a semi-upper class section. There was a four year old Honda in the drive.

He went to the door to call, "Buenos!" That was the same as knocking in the USA.

A rather pretty girl answered. He said he was Clint Faraday and asked to speak with Sr. Bouher. She opened the door and invited him in.

Inside, the house was truly luxurious. There were antiques and paintings and statuary. He was led to a den with more of the same. It had a big carved mahogany desk and a lot of modern computer equipment.

A thin dark man with flecks of grey in his black hair seated behind the desk waved to a seat.

Clint raised an eyebrow.

"I expected you. You are known as tenacious."

"You couldn't figure it was a bluff when that silly video showed her with that super ray gun from a Will Smith movie?"

"I was stupid not to see that. It is a good thing to know that no one has the weapon. That was a matter of the deepest concern to a great number of people."

"Someone does have the weapon. The Indios can have it at anytime they feel it to be necessary. There's one person who has several made because of this shit."

"Shit is what it is. Dr. Franken says it could be that or a highly directed laser, which can be reflected. I choose that explanation."

"I see. Perhaps I can arrange a demonstration that will prove it's no laser. We don't have nearly the capacity to make that small a hole at three miles. It would absorb tremendous power, which the Indios don't have. No one could make a directed laser at home."

"We have only the one person who claimed that, and he's most conveniently dead."

"You're rather stupid, aren't you? You didn't check with the police lab about their inspection of those holes in planes? From the middle of the comarca, where there isn't any major power generator? You think a few solar cells could power a laser that would do that at three miles?"

Bouher stared at the desk for a few seconds. "I'm no scientist."

"Neither is Franken if he says that could have been done with a laser."

"Dr. Franken says the crap about time distortion and gyroscopic effects and some kind of logarhythms is just that. Crap." He looked a little shocked.

"We knew about the bugs. We used them. *Part* of it *is* crap."

"Part of it?"

"Uh-huh."

"You know what the weapon is?"

"Me? No. JK does. He made a couple to test. He says the best way to throw what pass as scientists today off is to make a few ridiculous statements, along with a few simple facts. Determinant logarhythms? Bullshit! Reject the whole thing!"

Bouher stared at the desk again. "We have to stop this!" he whispered.

"You almost brought it," Clint pointed out. "You people who run the world through a lot of greedy schemes can't see that having more than a certain amount is always negative? What's the point? It's totally empty. You *know* that, but you keep on."

"You give away millions. You don't want something for yourself? For your children?"

"But we *have* it all! Can't you see that? We don't hide from anyone. We have friends. Actual, real friends. We hug when we meet. I care about them, they care about me. No one gives a shit about you, you don't give a shit about anyone."

"You don't make sense. Everyone wants more, wants control, wants power!"

"You're a dinosaur. You're about to bring about your own extinction, if you can't see what you are. I'm like the Indios. I pity you. It's all right here, but you can't see that.

"Are the idiot four part of you or just puppets you use?"

"I can buy as many thousand like them as I choose."

"Okay. That's all I wanted to know. Sit here and rot away

among all this fabulous art and money. It's for nothing. Those things have to be shared to have meaning. Your life is a huge shitpile of things that amount to nothing and you're not capable of seeing that.

"One warning. A way to bring the weapon out, fast, is to interfere with my people in any way. Wilam is dead because of your interference, if indirectly. If it was directly, you'd be dead now.

"I want to get back to my friends. I have them, you see. You can get back to sitting behind that desk trying to figure how to get more empty, meaningless things. I like to feel my life has some meaning. You don't have that. That's where it is. Goodbye."

He stood up and walked out. Bouher was staring at the desktop.

Back home. No more of this bullshit.

***

CD considered. Clint called and explained what had happened. The kids could all go back home. It was somewhen in the future, not now.

He called JK as soon as Clint said he was on the chopper, heading home. He explained what Clint had done. JK said he had done one thing that he would use. The weapon was things that were found around the house or garage. You could go to a garbage dump and get enough of most of it to build fifty of the things. All you needed past that was some copper wire and a battery of some sort.

They chatted. The families were having a lot of fun on the islands. He would tell them they could go back home, but were welcome to stay for as long as they liked. Things in the world actually were on the brink of crisis, but that's what those people manipulated the situation to be. They made so much *money* from it!

Page 62

CD rang off, sealed the jet, and headed for the island. It would be good to be there. He would leave the rest of the world to its own fate and problems.

JK

JK put a thing together from PVC pipe, some aluminum pie plates, a circular TV antenna, some capacitors and resistors he took from an old computer, and a neon light starter. It looked like a Rube Goldberg thing.

Psychology: Rube Goldberg's things always worked, if for silly reasons.

He took it out to a terrace and put the weapon behind it, extending through the center. He took a one inch thick piece of iron plating and put it against the wall, then went to the contraption to hook up a motorcycle battery to two copper wires that went to the device in the rear. The process from when he took the plate to lean against the wall was on unbroken video that followed him everywhere through a director on his belt.

He went to check the wiring, showing a tantilizing piece of the device, but not enough to actually show anything. He picked up a small round rock from a flower bed and dropped it into a piece of ½" PVC that extended above the back of the device.

He went back to stand in front of the device. to the side, where both the device and the plate were in the picture. He punched a button on a switch he had in his hand.

He went to the plate and showed the hole through it, holding it up so the sunlight showed it was all the way through, then went to the wall. It was constructed of rocks that were about two feet thick. He ran a piece of wire through the hole in the rock. It went all the way through.

He went back to turn the device off, then went inside to take the video recorder, recording the whole thing, to his computer room.

He had an unbroken cycle recorder on the video. There was no way it could have been faked.

He sat to make a voice recording that would explain everything except what the weapon was.

He added a warning at the end of it.

The house was done. It fit the place perfectly. It was simple, but complete.

Alma came from the orchid garden with Tyna. Nick and Janet came from the dock to stand with Clint and the others to look out over the water toward the comarca on the shore.

"We're here. Paradise," Janet said. They all agreed.

Nick's cellular rang. He answered, after saying he meant to get rid of that damned thing.

It was Pancho. He was back in Florida. Things were, if not great, a lot better than recently. The world situation had relaxed a bit. He thought it was because of something JK did.

Everybody had gone back to wherever their home was, except Tony and Shirley Jacobi, who decided they would spend half their time on JK's island and half elsewhere.

They all chatted with Pancho, then went inside, where Natalia and Yveth surprised them with a feast that would have cost five hundred dollars a plate anywhere else, if the ingredients were even available.

They lazed around for an hour, then went for a swim in the Caribbean, then rinsed in the river to return to the house.

Clint's phone rang, this time. He noted there were six missed calls. From Rojelio.

"Yo, Ro! Wa-apping?"

"Greetings, Clint. I have a small mystery here. A tourist who died when she fell off a small cliff. The problem is that there was no reason for her to be there.

"Would you care to investigate a bit?"

Clint didn't hesitate. "No."

C. D. Moulton's works are available on most major outlets as printed or e-books. CD writes the CD Grimes, PI mysteries, the Det. Lt. Nick Storie mysteries, the Clint Faraday mysteries, the Flight of the Maita science fiction series, books on orchid culture and many others of many types. Mystery, adventure, intrigue, science fiction, fantasy, paranormal, mild erotica, and factual.